Hunted

by

Elizabeth Kay

Illustrated by Dylan Gibson

v

You do not need to read this page – just get on with the book!

First published in 2009 in Great Britain by
Barrington Stoke Ltd
18 Walker St, Edinburgh, EH3 7LP

www.barringtonstoke.co.uk

ISBN: 978-1-84299-542-6

Printed in Great Britain by Bell & Bain Ltd

AUTHOR ID

Name: Elizabeth Kay

Likes: Snow, animals, travel.

Dislikes: Bony fish and bad drivers.

3 words that best describe me:
Arty, funny, energetic.

A secret not many people know:
I hated maths at school.

ILLUSTRATOR ID

Name: Dylan Gibson

Likes: Going out, walks, cycling, reading.

Dislikes: Sundays and Monday mornings!

3 words that best describe me:
Tall, talkative and hard-working.

A secret that not many people know:
I hate flying!

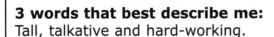

Contents

Chapter 1
Africa

"You don't get travel-sick, do you? That would be all I need," said Martin. Then everything tilted upwards, and the land dropped away below them.

Martin's my step-brother. He's 23, ten years older than me. He's studying elephants, and he doesn't talk about anything else. I knew he didn't want to take me to Africa with him, but my mum had to look after my gran, and my step-dad had to go to America.

"Elephants live as long as we do, and they are all very different from one another, just like people," Martin told me. "I've been following a herd of them, and making notes about what they eat."

I thought it sounded really boring. Elephants eat grass; what's so exciting about that?

"I want to see lions," I said. "Or a leopard."

Neither of us said very much for the rest of the flight. When we landed a man with very black skin was waiting for us, with a piece of card in his hand which read: *Martin Jones and Tim Morris.*

"Where's Kofi?" asked Martin.

"He could not come."

Martin looked surprised.

We followed the man outside to a battered old Jeep. The sun was right above us, and it was *hot*. So hot I nearly burned myself on the metal door-handle of the jeep. Martin got into the driving seat, and then we drove for hours and hours, past fields of maize and road-side huts. After a while we turned off down a track with deep bumpy ruts, but I still hadn't seen anything to get excited about.

And then, all of a sudden, I did.

As we came round a bend, there, in front of us, was a giraffe. I could hardly believe my eyes. It was huge. Martin put his foot down on the brakes, and the jeep slid to a stop and stalled. The giraffe moved off, graceful and clumsy at the same time, and vanished between the trees.

"That was a giraffe," I said.

"Oh, full marks Tim," said Martin in a sarcastic voice. "You could so easily mistake it for a rubbish-bin, couldn't you?"

"Look," I said, "you've been out here loads of times. I haven't. Give me a break, OK?"

"No, you look," replied Martin. "I was told to bring you out here."

"You didn't have to agree to it."

"Of course I had to!" shouted Martin.
"I couldn't afford to do this research without my dad's help. And now I've got to waste the summer baby-sitting."

I was so angry I couldn't think of anything to say. Baby-sitting? I'm 13. Martin started the engine again, crunched the gears, and drove the rest of the way to the research station without saying another word.

The building stood on wooden stilts by the side of a wide river. We went up some steps to a shaded balcony, which Martin called a veranda. "You're in there," said Martin, pointing to a door at the far end. "If you want dinner, it'll be about an hour."

The room was OK. I went over to the window, and looked out. There were hippos in the river, loads of them. When I visited the bathroom, something as long as a ruler with lots of legs ran across the floor, and out through one of the cracks in the wall.

I went out to the veranda. Martin was already there, drinking a beer with another man. "This is Noah," he said.

I laughed. It was a wind-up, it had to be.

Martin gave me a look, and I realised it wasn't. I told them about the leggy thing in the bathroom.

"That was a centipede," said Martin. "A nip from one of those really hurts. They're nasty."

"But not as nasty as the cobra I found under the jeep yesterday," said Noah.

I looked from one face to the other to see if they were joking.

They weren't.

I checked my room from top to bottom before I went to bed that night. There were a lot of strange sounds outside. Loudest of all were the croaks that sounded like a machine, or someone running a comb along the edge of a piece of paper, instead of their hair. It wasn't until I heard a clear *ribbit* that I realised they were frogs. After a while I got used to them – but just as I was dropping off to sleep I thought I heard something a bit different, far away. I sat bolt upright,

Chapter 2
Out in the Jeep

When I woke up the sun had only just risen above the trees, but already it was the pale yellow of a sun that baked mud and burned skins. The hippos had moved further up the river, and the water looked cool and tempting. I went down the steps to the river-bank, sat on the grass, and took off my shoes.

A few moments later I heard Martin come on to the veranda and say, "Maybe Kofi went back to his village."

I heard Noah mutter something.

Suddenly Martin said, "*What? You're kidding!*" Then he swore loudly and yelled, "Tim! *Tim!* What the hell do you think you're doing? Get back up here!"

How old did he think I was, five? I took my time, just to show him I wasn't going to be pushed around. Noah was laying the table for breakfast – glasses of red juice, rolls, coffee. None of it was going to spoil if I was a little late. "Where's the fire?" I asked.

"You stupid fool!" shouted Martin. He grabbed hold of my head, and turned it so that I was looking at the river. "What can you see?"

"Hippos," I said, though gritted teeth. "But they're miles away."

"Closer."

"Reeds ... a log of wood ..."

"That's a croc."

"Last year," said Noah, "a boy was eaten by a crocodile."

"You don't go anywhere, you don't touch anything, you don't even *breathe* without my say-so," ordered Martin, letting go of me. "OK?"

I glared at him.

"This isn't a back garden," he snapped. "People vanish."

"Like Kofi?"

Noah looked at Martin.

Martin said, "Kofi's gone back to his village for a few days."

You're lying, I thought. But now didn't seem to be a good time to come out and say it. "What's that?" I asked, pointing to the juice.

"Bissap."

"It looks like cough medicine."

"Don't drink it then," said Martin.

I took a tiny sip. It was OK.

"I need to follow up the elephant herd I've been studying," said Martin. "If you stay here you help get the lunch. If you come with me you take notes for me."

I didn't want to take notes, because I knew Martin would laugh at my spelling. But even that was better than peeling potatoes.

We drove back down the rutted track, and left the trees behind. It was much easier to see things. When a zebra ran across the road in front of us I shouted, "Zebra crossing!"

"I've heard that one so many times," groaned Martin. But he sounded a bit more friendly than he had before.

When we found the right herd Martin told each elephant apart by the notches in its ears, and I wrote down the names in the note-book. Most of the names were local, so it was OK to ask Martin how to spell them.

"Looks like two of the cows have gone walkabout," Martin remarked. "They're not here, anyway."

"*Cows?*"

"Female elephants, dumbo."

****

We spent the next two days doing the same thing, and we saw lots of different animals. Buffalos, antelopes, even a lion. I was so excited, even though it was a long way off. It had a sort of loose, easy stride, as though it could break into a sprint any second and cover the ground between us in no time at all. Scary. But scary in a cool sort of way, because I was in the jeep.

On the third day, we couldn't find the elephants at all. By mid-morning we'd only spotted some waterbucks and a few baboons, so we stopped for a drink.

I pointed at some tiny specks in the sky. "Are those vultures?" Martin handed me his binoculars, and the specks turned into birds.

"Could be a kill," he said.

"Lions?"

"Or a leopard. Or dogs."

"*Dogs?*"

"African wild dogs."

I put the water bottle back on the dashboard, and we set off across country. The jeep was open-topped, and Martin wasn't the best driver I'd ever met. All of a sudden, it didn't feel quite so safe.

Chapter 3
The Kill

There were hundreds of vultures. They were bobbing their horrible bald heads up and down and quarrelling. Between them, I could just see some grey skin, draped like a blanket made of leather across ribs the size of park railings. I turned to Martin. "It's an elephant, isn't it? What on earth can kill an animal as big as that?"

"Men," said Martin, tight-lipped. "Poachers." He drove the jeep right over to the half-eaten carcase, to scare the vultures away.

****

They didn't go very far. It was really hot out there in the open, and the smell was dreadful. I could see that the animal's tusks were missing. Martin saw me looking and said, "An elephant's tusks are made of ivory, and ivory is worth a lot of money. That's what the poachers were after. He turned to look at what remained of the elephant's ear. Then he picked up the radio and said, "They're back, Noah. They got Nalu. Any sign of Kofi?" There was a pause. "Right. We'll drive to his village then." He turned to me. "You OK about this? We may not get to eat for a while."

"Whatever."

Martin gave me a dirty look. It must have sounded as though I didn't care. I wanted to

say something, anything, to show Martin that I did care, because I did, but the words wouldn't come. I suddenly realised that I minded what he thought of me. It didn't mean I liked him, though.

My father left before I was born. Up until last year it had always been just me and my mum. Then my mum married Donald, and I hadn't liked that at all. But Donald had turned out to be really nice. His first wife had died, leaving him with just one son, Martin, who was away at university. When Martin and I finally met it was hate at first sight, but it had been easy to keep out of each other's way.

Until now.

Kofi's village was a mess of mud huts and breeze-block shacks. Chickens and cats and children ran around everywhere. Martin started talking to someone, and after a few moments he called me over.

"This is Kofi's brother. He hasn't seen Kofi, but it would be bad manners to leave without having dinner with him."

I gave a shrug. Martin gave me another dirty look, and I thought, *got it wrong again.* We all went and sat in the shade, under a tree, and drank cold water out of plastic cups. Several men came and sat with us, talking in a strange language. Martin seemed to get some of it, but not all, because he kept asking them to repeat things. They thought this was very funny.

When the food arrived Martin said, "Zambian sausages. You're in for a treat."

Zambian sausages turned out to be mice; gutted, boiled and dried. Martin had clearly had them before, and I watched. I couldn't drag my eyes away from him as he nibbled his way along the tiny little legs. He stripped away the rest of the flesh with his teeth, leaving just the head and the bones, which he threw to the dogs.

I went without.

"An elephant killed a man last week," said one of the villagers, in English. "We think he is the third man this rogue has killed."

"What's a rogue?" I asked.

"An animal who has gone to the bad. We call him Tusker, but no-one knows what he looks like. He trampled ..." He stopped, and went on to talk in his own language.

Martin nodded every so often, but he was looking worried. At last, he looked down at his watch and said, "We ought to go. We don't want to be out when the sun goes down, and we've got a good two-hour drive back."

Once we were on our way I said, "Why is it so important to be back by sunset?"

"Because whatever you may have seen on television, most animals hunt at night. As soon as the sun sets they walk in a different way, they slink. They turn into killers."

I looked round the jeep. "Don't you carry a rifle?"

Martin shook his head. "No need. I stick to the rules."

"Do you think Kofi was killed by a lion?"

"No, of course not."

"The rogue elephant?"

"No."

"What, then?"

Martin didn't speak for a moment. Then he said, "He may have run into the poachers. These men are the most dangerous animals of all, out here."

Chapter 4
Bad Luck

The herd of buffaloes was blocking the road. Martin jerked on the hand-brake, and tapped his fingers on the steering wheel as he waited for the animals to cross from one side to the other. The sun was sinking so quickly I almost felt I should reach out and catch it before it vanished. "We'll be all right in the jeep, won't we?" I said.

"Yeah, we should be. The only animals that seem to realise there are people sitting inside it are elephants."

At last the stragglers were across the road, and we could move. Martin turned on the head-lights, and the road in front was bathed with light. It made everything else to either side seem much darker. We drove for what seemed like ages. Then the jeep hit a bump, and I lifted right off the seat and bashed my elbow on the door as I landed.

Martin looked across at me. "Sorry."

"That's OK." I wanted to say, *keep your eyes on the road*. "That elephant," I said. "The rogue. What happened?"

"Dunno. The man who got trampled wasn't local – he could have been anyone."

"Why would the elephant have gone for him?"

"He'll have had a reason. Elephants are very clever. They have their own language. They use something called infrasound – it's too deep for us to hear. They can contact each other when they're miles apart. Did you know that in Sri Lanka, the elephants all turned round and went inland *four hours* before the Tsunami, the tidal wave, struck?"

I wasn't too sure I liked the sound of brainy leather-sided giants, who killed men for very good reasons of their own. What reasons could they possibly have? Self-defence? Revenge? "You know the night we first arrived?" I said. "I thought I heard a car backfiring. But it was the shot that killed that dead elephant we found, wasn't it? Nalu."

"Two nights ago? Yes, probably."

"Supposing Kofi *did* meet up with the poachers, the day before ..."

Martin turned to face me, really angry. "One thing you need to understand about life out here is that plenty of bad things happen without inventing more of them, and ..."

And that was when the wart-hog dashed out in front of us. Martin swerved, and we left the track altogether. The jeep bounced across the bumps and dips, only just managing to stay upright. All I could do was hang on, with every part of me tensed to breaking point. Then something loomed in front of us, and Martin battled like a madman with the steering wheel ...

There was a sickening jolt as we hit a tree. My knee slammed against the dash-board, and my jaws snapped together. I tasted blood. The engine started making a strange noise, so I leaned across and turned it off. Martin was just sitting there, his eyes closed, his head against the head-rest. One of the head-lights had gone out.

"Martin?"

No reply.

"Martin?" I was really scared now. I shook him by the arm. *"Martin."*

No response.

He's dead, I thought, *Mum will never forgive me.* Then I saw he was still breathing. There was a little trickle of blood on his forehead – he must have hit his head on the wind-screen, and bounced backwards.

OK, I thought, *now's the time to be sensible and to stay calm.* I didn't feel calm, though. I felt really frightened. There was a sort of tight feeling in my chest, and my fingers were tingling.

The first thing I tried was the radio, but I couldn't get it to work. If I waited for someone to come and find us, I might have a long wait because Noah would think we'd found Kofi and stayed the night at his village ...

I had no choice, really. I would have to *walk* back to the research centre. I wrote a note to say what I was doing, and left it on the dash-board. Then I covered Martin with a blanket. He moaned a little, although he didn't open his eyes. After that I put the Swiss Army knife in my pocket, and tucked the torch under my arm. I left the matches, so that he'd be able to read my message if he woke up. *When* he woke up. Then, taking a deep breath, I climbed down out of the jeep.

All I had to do was follow the road.

Chapter 5
Face to Face with a Leopard

The jeep had gone quite a long way. When I reached the track again I made a big arrow in the dirt with a stick, so that it would be easy to find. Then I started to walk.

It was the most scary thing I had ever done. How far was it, and how long was it going to take? I could hear the distant trumpet-call of an elephant. Was it Tusker, the rogue? Then a huge beetle landed on my arm, and I forgot all about elephants as I tried to brush it off. Its horrible feet clung to my sleeve, and its wings whirred like an electric fan. I dropped the torch as I tried to fend it off, and for a moment I was fighting an unseen enemy in the pitch dark. In the end the thing flew off, like an alien from a computer game, and I was able to pick up the torch again.

I wondered what my step-dad would say if Martin died. Would I get the blame? If I hadn't said anything about the poachers, Martin wouldn't have taken his eyes off the road and he'd have seen the wart-hog in time ... Please don't let him die, *please* ...

The moon came out, and I could see better. The longer I walked, and nothing happened to me, the more confident I became. When I'd been on the road for an hour I began to feel almost cheerful. Then I turned a bend, and came face to face with a leopard.

My heart seemed to stop, as though it had suddenly come across a sheer drop in front of it. My body wouldn't move, but my brain was racing. A few days before I had told Martin I wanted to see lions, or a leopard. But not like this. I was sure I could *smell* the animal, it was that close, sort of musky and oily, like unwashed hair. Was this how it felt to be hunted?

The leopard was just as surprised as me, though. It froze for a moment – then it hissed like an alley-cat, turned tail and fled. I started to shake and my knees felt rubbery and strange, the way they did in dreams when I found myself unable to move. I'd been less than a stone's throw away from a *real live leopard*; I'd seen the little white patches on its ears. I could see its pugmarks on the track in front of me. Martin had told me their footprints were called pugmarks.

Had he woken up yet? Would he see the note?

I was really frightened again now. I wanted to run, run all the way, but I knew that predators chase things that run. I had to carry on walking until this night-mare came to an end. I tried to think about something else. But I couldn't think about anything apart from man-eating leopards and spitting cobras.

The hour became an hour and a half. How much further? Three miles, maybe? I could just make out a herd of antelopes that Martin had told me were impalas, pale shapes in the moonlight. And then, suddenly, they were doing those graceful leaps like fairground horses on a merry-go-round. But they were running towards me, running away from something behind them. I froze. What was going to come out of the bushes – a lion? African wild dogs? Hyenas?

There was a sharp crack, and one of the impalas fell. The rest of the herd veered to the right and passed by me like ghosts.

What came out of the bushes were three men.

One of them spotted me, and pointed. I turned off the torch – but it was far too late, they'd seen me. I could just hear their voices, arguing with each other, despite the fact that they were almost half a mile away. I had a horrible feeling they could cover the ground a lot faster than I could.

Were they the men who had shot the elephant? Had they killed Kofi as well? Would they kill me, too? I wasn't going to wait around and find out, so I left the track and plunged into the bush. I would have to make my way back by another way.

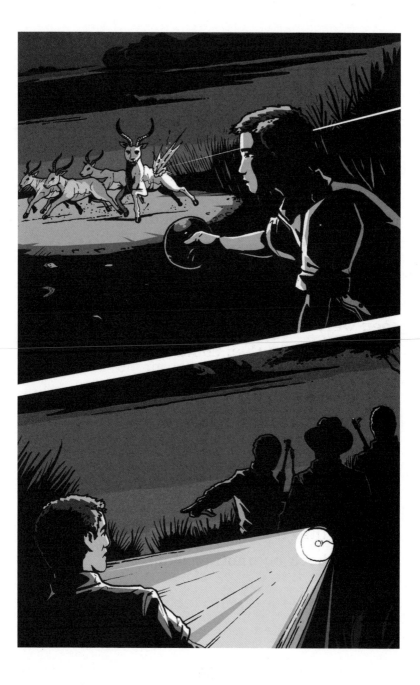

Chapter 6
More Bad Luck

The going was tricky in the dark. I didn't dare use the torch, and I had to focus really hard just to stay on my feet. After a while I stopped and listened. Zebras. Crickets. An owl.

And then, out of the blue, something hit me from behind, at the back of my knees. I went down like a sack of potatoes, and landed flat on my face. For a moment I just lay there, winded, my mouth full of grit, my heart racing, struggling to get air back into my lungs. Then someone poked me with the barrel of a rifle. I knew it was a rifle because I could smell the metal. I could smell my own sweat, as well; a cold trickle of fear.

"On your feet," said a man's voice.

I stood up, and turned to face the speaker. A flash-light swung round to point right at me, stopping me seeing anything. I shielded my eyes with my hand.

Another voice said, "We *cannot* take him with us. It is kidnapping. There will be big trouble, Mr Snyman."

For a moment no-one spoke. Then the one who must have been Mr Snyman said in a nasty voice, "Oh, *well done*. Now he knows my name."

"Very sorries, sir."

"You will be, Changa." Then the man jabbed me in the back and said, "Move."

I staggered forwards, and started to walk. Before long two of the men overtook me, carrying the dead impala between them.

"So what were you doing out here on your own, eh?" said Snyman's voice from behind.

I didn't want to answer him. Then I thought, Martin's back there, hurt. Maybe, *just maybe*, they'll help. "We crashed," I said. "My brother was driving, he needs help. I think he knocked himself out."

"Best way to be if a lion takes a fancy to you. And if you think we're going back to play Florence Nightingale, you've got another thing coming."

He's a white man, I realised, as the flash-light caught part of a jaw covered with ginger stubble the colour of fox fur. And then I thought – *I called Martin my brother.*

After what seemed like an age we turned downhill and found ourselves in a dry river-bed, hidden by over-hanging banks on either side. The next moment I heard voices and saw the flicker of firelight, and we arrived at their camp. One of the impala's legs was already roasting on a makeshift spit. Two elephant tusks were laid neatly on the ground, next to one another. A fourth man was tending the fire, and a fifth was sitting cross-legged on the ground. His hands were tied behind his back. His eyes opened wide with surprise and he said, "Tim Morris?"

I stared. "How did you know?"

"I should have met you at the airport."

"You're Kofi?" I felt like shouting for joy. "I thought you were ..."

41

"Dead," chipped in Snyman. "There's still time."

"Where is Martin?" asked Kofi.

"Crashed the Jeep," I said miserably. "He's badly hurt."

"Mr Snyman," said Kofi, "It is not too late to help …"

"Shut up," said Snyman, and he hit Kofi with the butt of his rifle. "We don't like Kofi, you see," he explained. "He used to be one of us. A poacher. Then he changed sides." He sat down and opened a bottle of beer.

The other three men kept busy stoking the fire, and getting the meal ready.

Kofi and I were the last to get something to eat and drink, long after everyone else had finished. Then Snyman ordered us both to get some sleep. It was clear that he didn't think I was much of a danger, as he didn't bother to tie me up. I lay down, using a lump of wood as a pillow, waiting for a chance to creep over to Kofi and cut him free ...

Chapter 7
Kofi

I opened my eyes. It was morning, and something was sitting on my feet. It bared its teeth at me, and began to chatter loudly. Then it ran off, carrying Martin's Swiss Army knife. I'd had my pocket picked by a monkey! I almost laughed out loud – how crazy was that? But actually, of course, it wasn't funny at all. There was no chance of cutting Kofi free now. I couldn't help wondering what Martin would say. Then I wondered if Martin was still alive.

A few minutes later, the poacher called Changa brought me a drink of water. Snyman was still asleep.

I went over to Kofi, sat down next to him, and gave him some too. Then, as no-one was watching, I slid my hand behind him and felt for the knot that held the rope around his wrists. I could only use the fingers of one hand, and the knot was really tight. The knife would have made things so much easier.

"I used to hunt bush-meat," Kofi said, to give me an excuse for sitting there.

"Bush-meat?" I asked, wiggling a finger through one of the loops of rope.

"Monkeys, mongooses, duikers ..."

"What's a duiker?" It was hard to keep my voice sounding normal.

"A little antelope, very good to eat."

"Oh."

Snyman turned over, gave a yawn and rubbed his eyes.

I haven't got long, I thought – then the first knot gave way. I started on the one beneath it.

"I was good with a bow and arrow," Kofi went on, "Mr Snyman got to hear of me, and he gave me a gun and told me to shoot at a tin can. Before long I could hit it every time. Then he told me that if I killed elephants for him, he would give me a lot of money."

The second knot was loose now.

"My mother was ill. We needed the money. She needed medicine. We do not become poachers because we are unfeeling people."

"But you're not a poacher now, are you?"

"No, because I have a proper job. I think that if Changa had such a job, he might come to care about the elephants as much as I do."

Snyman stood up. I wanted to scream. And then, quite suddenly, the rope slipped to the ground and Kofi was free.

"Act normally," said Kofi, under his breath.

Changa buried the ashes from the fire so that no-one could tell that anyone had been there, and Snyman picked up his rifle. "Our truck is a day's walk away," he said to me. "Once we've loaded the elephant tusks onto it, we'll let you go."

Kofi got to his feet. I saw that he'd wrapped the rope around his wrists again, so that it still looked as though he were tied up. Changa picked up a big backpack which, if the blood-stains were anything to go by, held some choice cuts of impala. The other two men hefted up the tusks on to their shoulders and they all moved off, in a line. Changa was at the front, and Snyman was at the back.

The climb out of the river bed was steep. Every fly in the area seemed attracted to Changa's backpack. I was so busy swatting them that I walked bang into Kofi, who was right in front of me, and I realised that everyone else had stopped.

There, blocking the path, stood the biggest elephant I had ever seen. Its tusks almost swept the ground.

"Out of the way!" yelled Snyman, raising his rifle.

No-one moved.

Snyman made an angry noise, and pushed me out of the way. Because the track was going uphill the poachers were right in his line of fire. Changa started to take off the

heavy backpack. The eyes of the other two stayed fixed on the elephant as, very slowly, they put the tusks on the ground. I was quite sure that the huge grey beast in front of me knew very well how the poachers had got them.

"It's Tusker," said Kofi in a whisper.

"How do you know?" I whispered back. "No-one's seen him."

"No-one apart from me," said Kofi. "I know him, and he knows me. When I say run, you must *run*. If you hadn't untied me I wouldn't have stood a chance."

Chapter 8
Tusker's Revenge

The moment the poachers let go of the tusks the elephant charged. Changa threw the backpack into Tusker's path, and ran. The other two sprinted towards us.

Kofi shoved me sideways, *hard*, and the elephant passed me by. I could feel the ground shaking through the soles of my shoes. On the track behind him lay a bloody, shapeless mass. The two who'd been carrying the ivory were running flat out, straight at

Snyman, who dodged to one side to get out of their way. The poachers dodged the same way and crashed into him, and all three men went down in a swirl of dust. Changa had shinned up a tree. So who was missing?

Kofi.

I felt sick. I wanted to look for him, hoping I'd been wrong but I couldn't take my eyes off Tusker. The elephant had stopped dead. With his foot, he nudged one of the ivory tusks that had been dropped by the men. Then he picked it up with his trunk and placed it by the side of the track. He ran his trunk over the other one, as tenderly as a mother comforting a child. Then he lifted that one as well, and put it next to the other.

The tangle of men in the dust started to unravel. The poachers struggled to their feet – but Snyman reached for his gun instead. There was a long, drawn-out moment as he

swung the barrel of the rifle round, and
Tusker went for him.

The crack of the shot and the scream
came together. Snyman flew through the air,
landed with a sickening thud on the ground,
and lay quite still.

Tusker turned to the poachers, as though
he were waiting for some sort of apology
from them. The bullet had missed him. The
poachers had run the wrong way, and they
were trapped. One of them threw himself on
the ground, and the other did the same.

"They are playing dead," said a voice in
my ear.

I turned to see who had spoken. *It was
Kofi*. I glanced back at the track, and realised
what the bloody mess was – the meat that
Changa had been carrying in his backpack.

"Sometimes playing dead will work with a young elephant who doesn't have much experience of life," Kofi went on. "But Tusker is neither young, nor inexperienced."

After a minute or two Tusker seemed to decide that he had had his apology from the two men on the ground. He walked across to Snyman's body, and touched it with his trunk. Once he seemed sure that the man was dead, he turned to look at the rest of us. Changa, above our heads in the tree, went very quiet. Tusker could have pulled it up, roots and all, as easily as picking a daisy. He was close enough for me to see the lines round his eyes, the hairs on his trunk.

"Hello Tusker," said Kofi in a low voice. "We meet again. But this time, I mean you no harm."

For a long moment, the elephant just looked at us. And then, quite suddenly, he backed off, and melted into the bush.

We carried Snyman's body to the nearest village, and Kofi rang the research station. He handed me the phone, a big smile on his face.

"Tim?" said a voice. "Is that you? Are you OK?"

"*Martin?*"

"You better believe it! You saved my life, with that arrow you drew in the road. That was how Noah found me."

"You're really OK? You were out cold, I thought you were dead at first ..."

"And I've got a sore head to prove it. *Hey.* I was worried sick about you, bruv."

"We'll be back tomorrow. And Martin – there's a man called Changa here, who wants to train as a game warden."

"You reckon he'd be good at it?"

Martin had actually *asked me what I thought*. A warm glow started up, somewhere inside me, although all I could say was "Yeah."

That evening, I asked Kofi how he'd known it was Tusker.

"I was there when he killed his first poacher," Kofi told me. "If you were an elephant, you wouldn't see Tusker as a rogue. You'd see him as a freedom fighter, trying to make the world a safer place for elephants. Now that Snyman's dead, he can go back to being an ordinary elephant."

But Tusker would never be just an ordinary elephant to me.

Barrington Stoke would like to thank all its readers for commenting on the manuscript before publication and in particular:

Liliana Billing
Benn Brown
Joanne Burgess
Rachel Burgess
Perry Capeling
Denny Casey
Kamran Chowdhury
Jacob Crampton
Sam Davis
Matthew Gasper
Justin Grant-Smith

Shellby Grayson
Ben Hancock
April Lloyd
Alwyn Martin
Lewis McKay
Toni Pardoe
Jay Pettitt
Ryan Price
Andrew Readle
Curtis Rowland
Andrew Shipley

Become a Consultant!

Would you like to give us feedback on our titles before they are published? Contact us at the email address below – we'd love to hear from you!

info@barringtonstoke.co.uk
www.barringtonstoke.co.uk